MW01140193

TO CATCH THE MOON

To dear Elli,
May your life be full of
light & joy.

Love,
anne-Marie J.

To Catch
the Moon

Written and illustrated by

Anne-Marie Grieder Jacobs

INKWATER
PRESS

PORTLAND • OREGON
INKWATERPRESS.COM

Jacobs, Anne-Marie Grieder.
    To catch the moon / by Anne-Marie Grieder Jacobs.
    pages cm
    SUMMARY: A little mouse, hearing a story about an
enormous ball of light, goes out into the world to try
to capture the moon.
    Audience: Ages 2-12.
    LCCN 2014911074
    ISBN 978-1-62901-116-5 (pbk.)
    ISBN 978-1-62901-117-2 (hbk.)

    1. Mice--Juvenile fiction. 2. Moon--Juvenile
fiction. [1. Mice--Fiction. 2. Moon--Fiction.]
I. Title.

    PZ7.J1485To 2014   [E]
                        QBI14-600117

Publisher: Inkwater Press | www.inkwaterpress.com

Paperback ISBN-13 978-1-62901-116-5 | ISBN-10 1-62901-116-9
Hardback   ISBN-13 978-1-62901-117-2 | ISBN-10 1-62901-117-7

Printed in the U.S.A.
All paper is acid free and meets all ANSI standards for archival quality paper.

1 3 5 7 9 10 8 6 4 2

In loving memory of my Daddy

Byron Harvey Jacobs

May this make you smile...

Thimble lived

with his family in a large, damp but cozy cellar. There was Mama, Papa, Grandpa, Grandma and his two sisters named Bobsy and Popsy.

Humans lived upstairs and kept fruit and food supplies in their cellar so there was always plenty for Thimble and his family to eat. The humans came down sometimes with a flashlight to get some food as the cellar was always dark.

Thimble lived a happy life in his cellar, but he was happiest when the light from the flashlight beamed down into the darkness of his home. He was fascinated with light and wished it could always be there.

One day his friend Scratch, a young rat who came to visit sometimes, told him about this enormous round ball of light in the sky, brighter than a thousand flashlights. He told his family about it, but no one believed Scratch. Thimble dreamed about this wonderful ball of light and could not get it out of his mind. He believed Scratch — he wanted so much to believe.

Thimble decided he was going to find this ball and show his family and friends so he told his parents one morning that he was leaving to get this ball for them so they would have a lot of light in the cellar. His family laughed at him and told him to stop day-dreaming and focus on trying to find food and just be satisfied because the darkness was where they lived and that was all there was.

So that night when everyone was in their soft, fluffy, cozy nest, Thimble tiptoed out of his hole and started his big adventure. He waited until the humans came down with their flashlight to get some supplies, then followed them up the stairs.

He was excited but scared at the same time. He tried to stay away from their giant feet and hoped they would not see him.

At the top of the stairs, the human he was following turned suddenly and he was blinded by the flashlight. His heart thumping, he hid in a crack of the stair, trembling. This was one of the first things Papa told him – hide from the humans. The human then walked into the house upstairs and opened the front door. Thimble cautiously followed him and hid under the porch. The human walked back into the house and closed the door. Thimble was now outside for the first time, all alone in the big world.

At first, there was only darkness. That first night he made a nest for himself with some dried leaves and during the day scurried quickly to find food. He lived like this for several days until he noticed one cloudless night a thin sliver of light in the sky. This was not the ball he was looking for, but he watched as night after night, this sliver grew and grew until one night, it was completely full — a glorious, bright ball of light, brighter than ten thousand flashlights! His heart almost exploded with joy.

Now he must catch it and
bring it back to his cellar.

He tried jumping as high
as he could, but he could
not jump high enough.

He tried
climbing up
the highest
tree he could
find, but it was
still too far away.

Discouraged, he sat down on a rock and thought he would never convince his family this wondrous thing existed. He turned around and was amazed to find the ball of light right behind him, in a large pool of water at his feet.

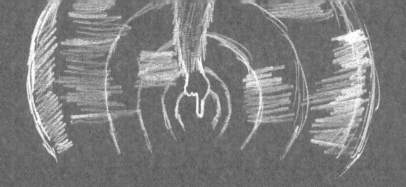

He stared in wonder and joy
and very gently put his paw
out to touch it. The water
rippled and the light danced
in waves around his paw.

His heart almost bursting with happiness, he ran back to the house and raced through a crack in the door, back into the cellar. He woke everyone up — his family was surprised and so happy to see him as they did not know where he had gone. He told everybody he had something wonderful to show them. They were so surprised that they followed him up the stairs, through the hallway, out the crack in the front door all the way to the pond.

There they finally saw this wondrous ball which they could touch and which rippled with dancing light. They were filled with wonder and joy.

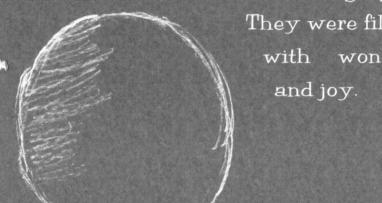

The light made Thimble's heart feel so full, that he did not need to catch this thing and bring it with him because it was already inside him. This light in him would brighten any space he would ever be in after tonight and he knew it filled his family's hearts too.

The End

Anne-Marie is an 11-year old living in Portland, Oregon. From a very early age, she was drawing and doodling at every opportunity, and continues to do so, especially in her math workbooks! This book was written and illustrated whilst she was in fifth grade. She has a passion for art and illustration, loves swimming, enjoys dance and plays the piano.

She shares her cozy "nest" with her mother and two sisters.

CPSIA information can be obtained
at www.ICGtesting.com
Printed in the USA
LVIC03n1106011114
411573LV00018B/76